# HERMAN NEEDS A HOME

For Hilary, who loved to read stories to her three grandchildren, who also loved to visit the sea and always managed to find the tiniest seashells. So Mum, this one is just for you xx
– *Lucy*

Thank you to Dan for your endless support, silly jokes and cups of tea.
– *Emma*

**Published by Brilliant Monsters**
**Brilliant Monsters Ltd**
**Registered Office:**
**15 Carew Road, Ealing, London W13 9QL**
First published 2022
001
**Text** Lucy Noguera
**Illustrations** Emma Latham
**Editor** Venetia Gosling
**Copyright** Brilliant Monsters Ltd

**Art Direction and Design by Accelerated Intelligence**
**Creative Director** Finbar Lenahan
**Designers** Hazel Thomson and Tom Camp

All rights reserved
The moral right of the author and the illustrator has been asserted
Printed and Bound in the UK

All rights reserved. No part of this publication may be reproduced or transmitted in any form or by any means, electronic or mechanical, including photocopying, recording, or any information storage or retrieval system, without prior permission in writing from the publishers. If you are reading this, thank you for buying our book.

The book is a work of fiction. Names, characters, places, incidents and dialogues are products of the authors imagination or are used fictitiously. Any resemblance to actual people, living or dead, events or locales is entirely coincidental.

A CIP catalogue record for this book will be available from the British Library.

www.brilliantmonsters.com

ISBN 978-1-9145770-1-7

# HERMAN NEEDS A HOME

LUCY NOGUERA

illustrated by EMMA LATHAM

Herman and Hiro are **hermit crabs.**
They live with their family around the
**rockiest rock pool** on the beach.

"My shell is too small,
I can't even **wriggle** my tail any more!"
moaned Herman to his little sister.

"**Mine too!**
I can't fit inside it to go to sleep!"
grumbled Hiro.

There was a new empty shell by the rock pool.
Hiro could smell it. She called out to her brother.

"Look Herman! I've found you a beautiful

"Sorry, it's just not **big enough** for me," Herman explained.

The crabs lined up in size order, from the **biggest** down to the tiniest!

"Ready,

steady,

GOOOOOOO!"

shouted Hiro.

Each crab took a turn
trying on the shells.

In and out they went, from

**one shell** to
**the next.**

"Look, Herman!"

Hiro was beaming. "My new shell fits
me just like a mermaid's tail!"

Herman was happy for Hiro but sad he didn't find a new shell for himself.

**"HIDE, HIRO!"**

shrieked Herman, rolling off the rock.

A beady eye loomed over them.
It belonged to the crabs'
scariest enemy!

"IT'S A

***HUNGRY SEAGULL!"***

squealed Hiro from inside her shell.

"KA CAW,

KA CAW,

KA CAW!"

The seagulls circled above them, ready to scoop up any stray little crabs for their dinner.

When the sea and the sky had turned a deep dark blue and the gulls had disappeared, the pair of crabs set off to find Herman a new shell.

They *scuttled* across the sand as fast as their tiny legs could carry them.

Herman and Hiro didn't find any shells, but they *did* come across a

**big, smelly**

pile of rubbish.

"Maybe one of these might fit?" said Herman, pointing at a can with his claw.

"Well, it *is* purple like my shell..." said Hiro.

"Oh no," said Herman. "It's far too

**scratchy**

and much too **sharp!**"

"Try this one,

it's fresh out of the sea!"

said Hiro, pointing at

a discarded bottle.

"It's too heavy," Herman groaned.
"And the water tastes sweet, not salty at all.
It's **horrible!**"

Hiro took a sniff.

"Eurggh!"
she agreed.

"How about this?" suggested Herman,

as he tried to SQUEEZE into an old snorkel.

"That looks about as cosy as living up
a swordfish's nose!" replied Hiro,
shaking her head.

"Urgh. This seaweed is

**disgusting!"**

spluttered Herman, spitting out a mouthful of rotten lettuce.

**"NOPE, NOPE, NOPE!**

– none of these are right!" said Hiro.

"Well, this is
definitely sandy...
and there's plenty of **s p a c e**," echoed
Herman's voice from inside a broken bucket.
"Maybe it's a bit **too big** though?"said Hiro.

"This FUZZY thing will just have to do for now,"
said Herman, yawning.
"I can't keep my eyes open a moment longer."
Hiro nodded. They needed to rest
before the sun came up.

A few hours later...

Herman, opened his eyes just as...

Herman felt his stomach lurch
as he flew up into the air!

“HIRO!”

shouted Herman.

# “I’M COMING!”

shouted back Hiro.

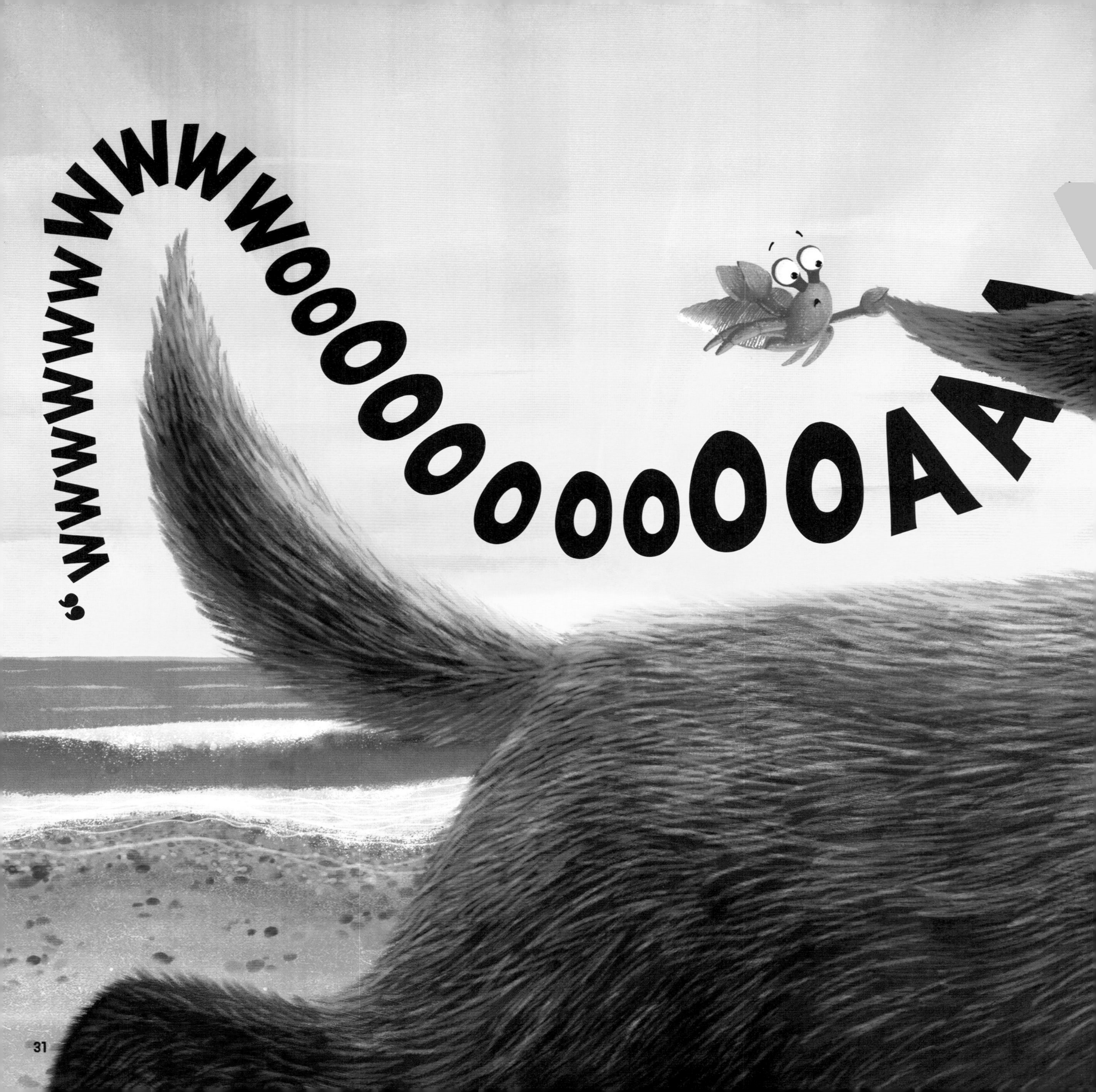

"WWWWWWWWWWWWOOOOOOOOOOOOA

AAAAAAHHHHHHHHH!"

The dog skidded to a halt
and dropped the ball onto
The Shell Cafe's decking.

THUMP! Boing!

"Ahhhhh!" yelled Herman.
"Ahhhhhh!" yelled Hiro.

The two crabs couldn't believe their tiny eyes.

"Look, Herman! There are

**so many shells!**

No wonder we couldn't find any on our beach – they're all here!"

Hiro snipped down the

**biggest,**

***fanciest***

**shell.**

"How does it **smell**, Herman?"
"Just like the **sea**!"

"How does it **sound**, Herman?"
"Just like the **waves**!"

"How does it **feel**, Herman?"
"It feels...

…just like

# HOME!”

# DID YOU KNOW?

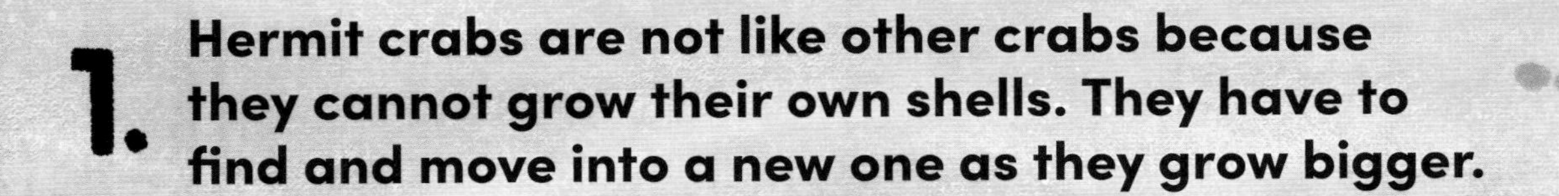

1. Hermit crabs are not like other crabs because they cannot grow their own shells. They have to find and move into a new one as they grow bigger.

2. Hermit crabs have been found living inside plastic lids, cans or other pieces of rubbish instead of shells as beaches become more polluted.

3. Across the world around one million plastic bottles are used every minute. Plastic bottles can last for around 400 years!

4. There could be more plastic than fish in the oceans by the year 2050.

## What can we do to help?

**Rethink** – what do we actually need?

**Refuse** plastic wherever you can.

**Reduce** the amount of plastic you use.
Single use plastics are only recycled 9% of the time.

**Reuse** items whenever you can.

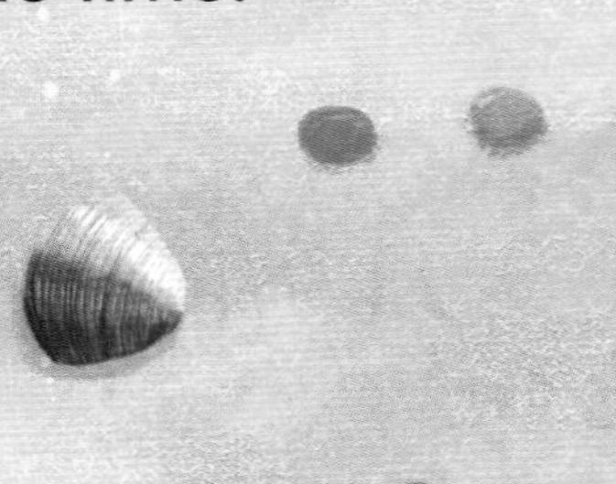

**Recycle** as much as possible.

***Thanks to the WWF—World Wildlife Fund.***

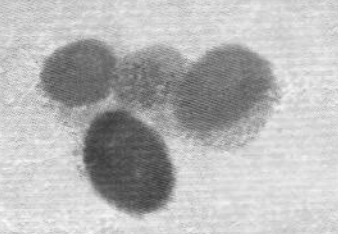